O, let me find some day
Before I go,
One little scrap of truth
That I may *truly* know.

It need not be a blazing sun
On worlds to shine;
A candle stub would do,
If it were mine.

Sarah Osgood Grover

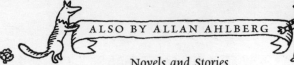

ALSO BY ALLAN AHLBERG

Novels and Stories

The Bear Nobody Wanted
The Better Brown Stories
The Clothes Horse
The Giant Baby
The Improbable Cat
It Was a Dark and Stormy Night
Jeremiah in the Dark Woods
My Brother's Ghost
Ten in a Bed
Woof!

Verse

Friendly Matches
Heard it in the Playground
The Mighty Slide
Please Mrs Butler

THE BOY,
THE WOLF, THE SHEEP
AND THE LETTUCE

A Little Search for Truth* by
ALLAN AHLBERG

with illustrations by
JESSICA AHLBERG

PUFFIN

---

*Or a rigmarole perhaps

PUFFIN BOOKS

Published by the Penguin Group
Penguin Books Ltd, 80 Strand, London WC2R ORL, England
Penguin Group (USA), 375 Hudson Street, New York, New York 10014, USA
Penguin Books Australia Ltd, 250 Camberwell Road, Camberwell, Victoria 3124, Australia
Penguin Books Canada Ltd, 10 Alcorn Avenue, Toronto, Ontario, Canada M4V 3B2
Penguin Books India (P) Ltd., Community Centre, Panchsheel Park, New Delhi – 110 017, India
Penguin Group (NZ), cnr and Airborne and Rosedale Roads, Albany, Auckland 1310, New Zealand
Penguin Books (South Africa) (Pty) Ltd, 24 Sturdee Avenue, Rosebank 2196, South Africa

Penguin Books Ltd, Registered Offices: 80 Strand, London WC2R ORL, England

www.penguin.com

First published 2004

1

Consultant Designer: Douglas Martin

Set in dpTYPE Rialto

Printed in England by Clays Ltd, St Ives plc

British Library Cataloguing in Publication Data
A CIP catalogue record for this book is available from the British Library

ISBN 0-141-38069-1

CONTENTS

AUTHOR'S NOTE

My name is John Smout. I am — LORD HELP ME — a writer of children's books. I have written a few in my time; not few enough, some say. Full of low comedy and foolishness, most of 'em. (Good illustrations, though.) Now, however, as I begin to descend the hill of life, I feel the urge to set down something halfway . . . sensible. Yes, sir, mature work, that's what I'm aiming for; a little SEARCH for truth.

This book required much toing and froing on the author's part and never would have reached its end (or ends!) without help. Thus, thanks are due to Mrs McFirkin for her unstinting hospitality and free firewood, 'Grandma Pumfrey' (my saviour with a shotgun) and little Rosalind McFirkin for access to her remarkable diary. The Book of Courage (Edwin Osgood Grover) and The Paradox Box (Redstone Press) jointly supplied many of the quotations used herein. (I like a good quote.) The Collected Poems of Sarah Osgood Grover, sister to Edwin, have been my constant inspiration. To my old mum, MOVER of WARDROBES, I dedicate this book.

J. T. S.
March '04

[1] The Boy, the Wolf, the Sheep and the Lettuce

I have never but once succeeded in making G. E. Moore
tell a lie and this was by a subterfuge. 'Moore,' I said,
'do you always speak the truth?' 'No,' he replied.
I believe this to be the only lie he had ever told.

Bertrand Russell

You may think you know this story, it has become famous after all, but I am here to tell you now you DON'T know it. No, sir – no y'don't. Don't argue.

Y'see, what most boys and girls (I guess you're one or the other), what most people know is only the boy's version, farmer's boy supposedly, though he never was. Well, for starters even this version is not up to much, and in any case there are OTHER POINTS OF VIEW.

But there you are. We think we know, and we don't know. We think we don't know, and we do. Lies, confusion, *subterfuge* etc. are all around us. Not to worry. I am here to sort it out, lead you through the maze, so to speak. You can rely on me.

P.S. There's a girl in the book too; it's not all boys. Oh, yes, and one other thing. If your parents or teachers, they're a nosy lot, ask what you're reading, tell them it's educational. Intellectual. Yes, tell 'em you're reading Bertrand Russell.

So, here it is, the famous version, the one we all know. As I've explained, it's not the whole story, the whole truth (Your Honour), not by any means. But it will do to be going on with, set the wheels in motion, so to speak, set the ball rolling, set the scene, set the jelly (no – not that). Anyway, here it is:

THE BOY, THE WOLF, THE SHEEP AND THE LETTUCE

Once, not so long ago, a farmer's boy had to deliver a wolf, a sheep and a lettuce to a nearby town. By and by he came to a river which it was necessary to cross in a boat. Unfortunately, the boat was only big enough to take the boy and one other at a time. The problem was, he couldn't leave the wolf alone with the sheep because the wolf would eat the sheep.

He couldn't leave the sheep alone with the lettuce because the sheep would eat the lettuce.

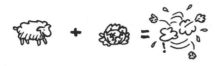

So the question is, how did the boy get all three of them and himself over the river to the other side?

Well, 'easy-peasy', I hear you say. We all know that, or think we do. The boy – you remember – the boy takes the sheep over first and then comes back and takes the . . . and so on. And so on. But – and this is the point I want to make – this version is just that, a version, and not much of one either. For a start there's almost no detail, is there, likely to persuade us, any of us – man, girl, chicken even – that THIS IS WHAT HAPPENED. For instance, why only one lettuce? What use is a single, solitary lettuce? At least let's have a pack of three. And (this is one for the grown-ups) what sort of parent is it who sends their child off all alone to deliver some monstrous great wolf to . . . anywhere?

But you must forgive me – Oh, dear! – I get worked up at times.* It's the sheer preposterousness of some so-called stories that agitates me, blows me off course and, er . . . makes me forget what I was going to say.

What was I going to say? Where was I? Oh, yes. The point is, y'see, there could be other versions. There must be. There are! Yes, sir, and I am here to tell you now . . . er, all of 'em. Starting with the boy himself, young Percy.

---

* I'm an occasional SHOUTER.

[2] The Boy's Version

Father, I cannot tell a lie. I did it with
my little hatchet.*

George Washington

I have talked to this boy, or rather listened
to him. He's a bit of a chatterbox, no shortage
of detail here. This is a simplified version – he's
a bit of an exaggerator too – of what he says,
what he *claims* happened. It's a version all right,
but keep that pinch of salt handy.

The boy's name was Perseverance McFirkin, a
ridiculous name, I'll grant you, but what passes
for normal in our part of the world. (Wait till
you hear the wolf's name. Wait till you hear the
lettuce's!) The boy, as mentioned earlier, was not
a farmer's boy at all, he was a woodcutter's boy
and his mother was the woodcutter. His father
was a partner in a window-cleaning business.

So here we are on the day in question, early

---

on a bright and fragrant morning, with mari-golds blooming in the window box and little larks out on the sill. Young Perseverance arose from his bed, washed his face, ate his breakfast and attended half-heartedly (he was reading a comic) to his mother's instructions.

'Now Percy,' she said, 'I require you to get dressed and run a few errands. Take this lettuce to your Auntie Joyce, this sheep to Mr Bodley – Oh yes, and drop this wolf off at Grandma Pumfrey's.' Grandma Pumfrey was the local vet. What business a wolf had with a vet, you will presently hear.

'Yes, Mother,' said Percy. Whereupon, up he leapt and away he flew, like a pip from an apple, according to him. Up the stairs to throw some clothes on. Out into the yard to hitch up the donkey. Round to the front of the house, plus donkey, plus cart for loading:

lettuce
sheep
wolf
football boots
fizzy drink
comic.

Kiss for his mother, blown kisses for his little sister (told you there was a girl), still in her nightie and waving at him from an upstairs window, brisk 'Giddy-up!' for the elderly and somewhat deaf donkey, thence through the gate,
down the cowtrack,
round the bend and off . . .
into the forest.

The FOREST. This boy had much to say about the forest. It was his favourite place, apparently. A place of ancient trees and clearings – flickering sunlight – high winds – snow at times. A place of tigers and bears, according to him, and bandits. I see from my notes that he was in the forest for twenty minutes or so and that it took him three quarters of an hour to tell me about it.

But let us move him on. The road through the forest to the town rose and fell with the contours of the ground. From time to time little racing streams cut across it. It was the width of a cart, no more. (You must hope on your journey not to meet one coming the other way!) The boy sat up on the cart, whistling. On his left, in a wooden tray, the Lettuce; on his right, with his lead – yes, lead – wrapped round the iron frame of the seat, the Wolf. And in the bed of the cart, curled up on an old blanket and gazing back the way they had come, the Sheep.

Actually, to be fair to this boy, to Percy, this is his version after all, let me quote a little from his actual words. It is not necessary to believe everything he says, though some of it, surely, is likely to be true.

'It were an easy trip' (he has an open, smiling face, gingerish hair, freckles), 'I were never scared. I know that old forest.' He whistles at this point. 'Seen a polecat up a tree – I never minded it. Seen a bandit or a robber or somebody, off in the trees.' Whistles. 'Stood up in the old cart and picked me a pear off a pear tree. Seen another man with an eye patch and a wriggling sack. I never minded.' Whistles.

'But what about your companions?' I asked. 'Can you tell me anything about them?' I didn't want to put words into his mouth, you understand. It was the TRUTH I was after. In any case, his mouth was fairly well full of words as it was.

'Well, see, that sheep I was taking to Mr Bodley, it were *his* sheep. The Wolf was going to Grandma Pumfrey's. I was supposed to leave him there and my dad would pick him up after. I had it all writ down. See, he needed his claws clipping, his teeth scraping – a build up of tartar or something – and his booster wolf-flu jab.'

'But a wolf –' I could hardly contain myself, '– to a vet?'

'Oh, he were some old wolf. Tame enough. I was never scared of him. Not like the tigers. See, the tigers –'

'What about the Lettuce?'

'The Lettuce was for Auntie Joyce, I forget

what for. Don't believe she was supposed to eat it, though. There was something else. I forget.' Whistles.

On went the cart (we will get there) with its effervescent boy, patient donkey and UNLIKELY PASSENGERS. By and by the trees thinned out and the track widened. Small fields appeared (broccoli mostly), the odd cottage, telegraph pole, bus stop. Then, straight ahead and glittering under the rising sun, the river. And beyond the river, right up against its further bank, the green slate roofs and smoking chimneys of the town.

There was a bridge which was closed off, on account of an unfriendly, blackmailing troll, according to Percy, but it was roadworks, really. I checked it out.

'So how did you get across?' I asked. 'Was there a boat?'

'There was – a ferry boat. Warn't there, though – disappeared – and the ferryman – and his missus. Kidnapped, I heard, or gone on holiday, somebody said.'

'So what did you do?'

Percy smiled, and I saw that he had a tooth

 missing. 'I *Percy*-vered!' he cried. (An old family joke, apparently.) 'That's what I done. Found this titchy little boat with a paddle – like a tennis bat.'

And thus the tale, or the disentanglement of the tale, as it were, continues. Young Perseverance McFirkin, in the peace and solitude of his own orchard at the side of the house, in the swing and serenity of his own hammock stretched out between two plum trees, expands on and delights in his own cleverness – coolness – presence of mind. (I sit there, taking notes.)

'I think to m'self, this'll do it. I'll take 'em over one at a time. Only trouble was –' He flicks a moth away from his nose. 'Only trouble was, I couldn't leave the Wolf with the Sheep, and I couldn't leave the Sheep with the Lettuce. Tricky that.'

But solvable, apparently, for what young Percy did, or so he says, was grab his old wood-cutter's axe (or hatchet) out of the cart, chop a few trees down and make himself a raft. Found a pole. Drove the donkey plus cart onto the raft . . . and floated over. And the Sheep fell overboard and he rescued her. And a crowd gathered on the further bank with much cheering. And the Wolf, Sheep, Lettuce all got to where they were supposed to. (I am rushing a bit here. We had been in that orchard half a day, my notebook was full and it was getting dark.) And (too many 'ands', sorry about that)* Percy played football, and scored, you guessed it, the winning goal. Had tea at his friend's house, spent the night at Auntie Joyce's . . . and slept the sleep of the just, whatever that means.

---

*Too many brackets too – Oh, dear.†

---

†Too many 'toos' – aaargh!

p.s. All in that rush there at the end, and in my natural eagerness to REACH THE END, I must confess I skipped a couple of things. Allow me to rewind a little. As I mentioned, it was darkening in the orchard. Pinholes of starlight appeared to hang in the branches of the trees. The earlier heat of the sun, soaked down into the earth, was rising up again full of the smells of fallen fruit and grass. Percy was expanding on his heroics in that river crossing. The Sheep was overboard, the brave boy poised to rescue her.

I should add that Percy's little sister had joined us at this time, back in her nightie again, ready for bed and up there in the hammock with him. Anyway, Percy was telling his tale. I was sat there in a folding camp chair. Rosalind, that was his sister's name, was dangling her chubby little legs over the edge of the hammock. The rescue was in progress, yes, the crowd cheering. And then . . . a movement in the shadows. A cough. A voice. 'Not true,' it said, so deeply and yet quavering too. 'A fiction altogether. I am the *best* of swimmers.'

[3] Currants from a BUN

A lie can be halfway round the world before
the truth has got its boots on.

Old Dutch Proverb

There we have it: the boy's version, and much
good may it do us. It is as full of holes as
a Swiss cheese, a sieve, a MOTH-EATEN OLD
. . . something or other. Carpet. I mean, he has
given us all this STUFF (hardly a tenth of what
he told me) and you'd require to pick the truth
out of it, if there was any, like currants from a
BUN.

Oh, dear, I am getting carried away again. I
can feel it. I mean, I ask you: bandits – tigers –
TROLLS. All that business with the raft. I have
been to the river, both banks. Searched high and
low. There is no raft. That boy, that Percy – is
Perseverance really his name, I am beginning to
wonder – has a truly (!) vivid imagination. Or
as his little sister was later to say, 'That Percy, he
is a big fibber.' I would scarcely trust him to tell

me what socks he was wearing. There again, on the other hand (or foot), the Wolf, the Sheep and the Lettuce, that bit's true, sort of. I mean, they WERE in the cart and he DID take them.

Incidentally (I should've mentioned this earlier), this text, these pages you are presently (pleasantly?) reading, is based on a mountainous amount of notes made within a week or so of the alleged events, interviews mostly, with the participants themselves. The book itself, however, has taken much longer to complete. I am a slow worker. Sometimes days passed when all I had to show was minus fifteen words, crossed out, that is, from the day before. Such is the writer's lot.

Let's move on.

[4] The Sheep's Version

UNCLE EDITH
This poem, I regret to say
Is quite untrue.
Uncle was really Auntie, of course
And Edith, actually, Hugh.

Allan Ahlberg

'I am the *best* of swimmers.'
Yes, I expect you worked it out, it was the Sheep back there in the orchard. Her creamy fleece half luminous in the dark. Her mild face with its surprising glint of spectacles. Her woolly (?) scarf.

We did not talk much at that time, the Sheep and I. It was late, I was weary. Percy, I may say, was yet full of beans, nattering on there in his hammock with no more audience than a couple of moths and a hedgehog.

The following day began with a colossal downpour. For a whole hour I stood up at my bedroom window watching grey curtains of rain sweep in above the trees. The rain bouncing up from the patio slabs, the table and chairs, the mower. Another hedgehog's progress along the shrubbery. My beloved roses swaying and glowing even then in the gloom.*

It was late afternoon before I was able to return, by mud-splattered bicycle, to the McFirkins' place. I sought the Sheep out where she sheltered, snug and dry, in a corner of the barn. With some reluctance – there were secrets here as well as lies, she implied – she nevertheless embarked upon her version of events.

So here we are again on the day in question, early on a bright and fragrant morning (no disagreement there). Sunlight slanted across the house, the barn, the paddock. In the paddock – dew on the grass, cornflowers and buttercups – one VERY IMPORTANT SHEEP was safely grazing. A journey was necessary. The Sheep must be transported, with the utmost care and no delay, to Professor Bodley's. The McFirkin boy received his instructions. The Sheep was brought

---

*The sun declines yet light still glows
 Below the hill, inside the rose.
                    Sarah Osgood Grover

into the cart, made comfortable on a pile of blankets. The journey began.

The Forest. The Sheep had little to say about the forest. She was no devotee of trees, preferred an open field – hedgerows – sky. In response to my enquiries, she confirmed that it *was* 'Professor' not 'Mr' Bodley (actually, it turned out 'Doctor' was a possibility – Ha!), and that, as it happened, though no concern of hers, there was a wolf and a lettuce in the cart too. Naturally, I pressed her on this matter.

'What can you tell me about the Wolf?'

'He was a wolf.'

'A tame one?'

'Hardly. He was *common*.'

'And the Lettuce?'

'I scarcely noticed it.'

Truth is, she was eating what might well have been a lettuce when I first arrived in the barn. Tucked it out of sight as I came in.

The forest part of the story, so said the Sheep, was boring, bumpy and slow. The boy – Percival? – had an irritating inclination to whistle. The Wolf kept giving her looks.

'What sort of looks?'

'Wolf looks.'

'Were you, er . . . worried?'

'No. Yes. Sometimes.'

The Sheep fell silent and stared studiously (it was the spectacles) about her. More rain was rattling on the roof of the barn. High up, suspended from a beam, a family of sleepy bats was twittering and squeaking. A lone cat sat in the open doorway looking out.

I endeavoured to keep things moving.

'Did you see any bandits at that time? Any tigers?'

'No, not a one.'

'A polecat maybe. A man with a wriggling sack?'

'No.' The Sheep shook her head. 'Saw a squirrel – a multitude of mushrooms. Saw a milkman. Hm.'

On went the story, eventually, and the cart with it. Out of the forest, along the wider road, dipping and swinging, with tantalizing smells of clover and cut grass (no broccoli?), down towards the river.

And YES there was a bridge, and YES it was closed off, who knows why. And YES AND YES there was a pier – no ferryman though, or 'missus'. No ferry boat.

So now we come to it again: the river crossing. Actually, consulting my notes, I note (!)
that this was the part the Sheep chose to tell first.
Eager to contradict Percy's account, I suppose.
As you can see, I have rearranged things chrono-
logically. This tale is tangled enough as it is.

On the subject of these notes, I should point
out that even they are not always one hundred
per cent reliable. There's a page here, for
instance, all smudged with rain; a couple of
others almost shredded (claw marks – I will
explain later). And, of course, they are, after all,
just notes, brief records or summaries set down
to assist the memory.

Except – and this is the point I want to make
– Oh, Godfrey, it's taking an ETERNITY
though for me to make it. Words do have a mind
of their own, don't they? We struggle and sweat
with all our might (some of us) for clarity –
simplicity – concision. Yet somehow, time and
time again, it all just gets away from us, and we
are left . . . *bamboozled*. Yes, that's the word.

Where was I?

The Sheep. The point is, in her case the notes
really are reliable. She talked in notes, little

telegrams, all the time. Getting her to put ten words together was a triumph. Percy, you could say, made it up and said too much. The Sheep kept it to herself and said too little. The end result, in my opinion, was the same: DECEP-TION. But never fear, rely on me. They cannot keep us in the dark forever. We will unravel this tangle yet.

So CLARITY, SIMPLICITY, CONCISION:

1 With no bridge and no ferry boat, Percy makes use of a canoe he's found.

2 The canoe will accommodate only Percy himself and one other at a time. No problem, in the Sheep's opinion. Simply take her over, utmost care, no delay, and leave the others behind.

3 Percy thinks differently. He takes the Sheep over first and goes back for the Lettuce.

4 Realizes he can't leave the Lettuce with the Sheep, returns with the Lettuce and goes back with the Wolf.

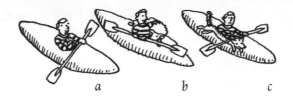

a   b   c

5 Realizes he can't leave the Wolf with the Sheep, returns with the Wolf and goes back for the Sheep.

6 Sits on the bank with the Wolf, the Sheep and the Lettuce.

7 Scratches his head . . . and reads a comic.

8 Whistles.

Naturally at this point I asked again about the raft. Here, more or less word for word, is the exchange that followed:

'Could you say a word or two about the raft?'

'Yes: *no . . . raft.*'

'Percy tells me he took (I consult my notes), he took his little axe and –'

'No little axe.'

'Ah!'

'Little fibber – little shrimp.'

'I see.'

'Could not chop his way out of a paper bag.'
(Ten words.)

'I see, of course. So, er . . . no rescue then?'

'Told you that already.'

'No crowds – hm? No cheers?'

Silence from the Sheep.

By this time the rain had stopped for good. Dazzling rainbowed light, refracted from the puddles, bounced back and up into the barn through the open doorway. Soft waves of straw dust, hay dust, bat dust for all I know, swirled in the brighter air. Outside, children's voices, yelling and laughing, and the thud of a ball.

The Sheep was becoming grumpy. She had a secretive nature, I realized, and disliked being questioned. Even so, I pressed on. (How else to sort things out?) If there was no raft, if Percy merely sat on the bank and read his comic, as the Sheep suggested, how in blazes *did* they get across? Because they did. That much is known; half a dozen witnesses at least confirmed it; confirmed their arrival, that is, if not the crossing itself.

The Sheep frowned. Well, it was no thanks to Percy, according to her. It turned out not only did he read his comic, drink his fizzy drink, kick his football, he fell asleep as well. '*Without help,*' (pay close attention to this), 'Without help,' the Sheep declared, 'we'd still be there.'

Whereupon, in one of those coincidences good stories are supposed to avoid, the football itself came flying through the doorway, scared the cat, bounced off a barrel and caught the Sheep a glancing blow on the side of her head. Which was rotten luck for all concerned, except the ball. The Sheep acquired a muddy patch on her otherwise spotless fleece, her glasses were undamaged though, and I lost any chance of continuing my investigations. What help? . . . Who from? . . . And when? . . . And where? . . . And . . . Oh, botheration, how exasperating.

The Sheep rose to her feet and huffily, peevishly, silently departed. Meanwhile, Percy and his little sister came charging into the barn, all smiles and greetings, recovered the ball and charged out again. I packed my bag and trudged off. Mrs McFirkin was across the yard, pegging washing out. Sensing my dejection, perhaps, though she was a kindly soul in any case, she invited me onto the veranda for a cup of tea. Presently, up rushed Percy, eager to show off his latest acquisition, a bowlful of little frogs, and tell me his latest adventure. Came down in the rain, they had. Sucked up by a waterspout, he wouldn't wonder. Caught 'em in his hat. And Rosalind, perched up on her mother's knee with a biscuit, mouthed a single silent comment of her own in my direction.

'Fibber!'

[5] Space, Time and Grandma Pumfrey

Anyone who isn't confused doesn't
really understand the situation.*

Ed Murrow

Clarity, Simplicity, Concision – yes. On the other hand, Confusion, Mystery, Doubt. I mean, what are we to make of things so far? According to Percy, he drives the cart to the river, constructs a raft and delivers the Wolf, the Sheep and the Lettuce to their destinations.

> i.e. The Wolf to Grandma Pumfrey's
> The Sheep to Mr/Prof/Dr Bodley
> The Lettuce to Auntie Joyce

According to the Sheep, it's mainly – utmost care, no delay – the Sheep who's delivered. There's no raft but there is a canoe. Which is no use because

---

*

Percy can't work out how to get them over one at a time. Percy dozes off on the bank and without some mysterious HELP, which the Sheep declined to CLARIFY, they'd all still be there.

The Sheep appears more trustworthy than the boy. On the other hand (how many hands is that?), she's also more secretive, and (have you noticed?) inclined to enlarge her own role in the story, i.e. a bit of a bighead. Later on, for instance, when she heard this book might eventually be published, she proposed in all seriousness her own alternative title: *The Very Important Sheep*.

Hm. Where was I? Ah, yes, on the veranda.

I remained at the McFirkin place for a couple of hours. My cup of tea was accompanied by delicious home-made biscuits. Later on there was pork pie, tomatoes and a Scotch egg. When Mr McFirkin showed up, on *his* mud-splattered bicycle (plus bucket and ladder), there was delicious home-made beer and introductions.

'Here's Mr Smout, the writer, dear – come to see us!'

And, 'This is my husband . . . Hermann.'

Mrs McFirkin, it turned out, was a great reader with a high regard for authors, yours truly included, or even in particular. The children, of course, had never heard of me.

Anyway, such HOSPITALITY. I live alone, you see, or did in those days. Simply to have a PLATE brought to me with FOOD upon it and a mug of FOAMING beer, was a huge relaxing pleasure. It did, however, I must confess, undermine my determination to question Mrs McFirkin in particular about the activities of her son, the movement back and forth of the Sheep, the odd (to put it mildly) business with the Wolf and the whereabouts of the Lettuce. Though I did try.

Mrs McFirkin was tall, wide and strong, a wonderful woodcutter, if somewhat vague and dreamy at times. She loved, of course, her little boy to bits, and his little sister likewise. The possibility that there could be any flaw in his nature was for her an impossibility. Thus she confirmed that Percy *had* left the house (on that bright and fragrant morning) with his unlikely load: Lettuce to the left of him, Wolf to the right, Sheep to the rear. And so on, and so on. Completed his assignments. Slept the night at Auntie Joyce's. Come home safe and sound.

The Lettuce, Mrs McFirkin explained, was her

own prize candidate in the horticultural show: salad section. The Sheep belonged to (let's call him 'Professor', shall we, for sanity's sake), to Professor Bodley. He paid the McFirkins to lodge and supervise the Sheep from time to time in their clover-rich paddock and feed her extra vitamins.

The Wolf – Ah, here we come to it – the Wolf was, er . . . Mrs McFirkin hesitated (embarrassed, guilty perhaps?), a hesitation soon reinforced and extended by the arrival of her hot and thirsty husband, the bedtimes of her children, washing up of crockery, blowing of nose. Etc.

Well, it was a tough question to put to so soft-hearted a mother whose hospitality you're still enjoying: 'How could you send your little boy off all alone through the forest WITH A WOLF?'

Yes, a tough question. I never asked it.

Thus, eventually, the shadows lengthened across the yard, the bats came skimming out of the barn, the forest itself gave every appearance of creeping up on the well-lit, cosy house . . . and I departed.

* * *

The Sheep. Before completing my journey home through the darkening forest, I ought, I think, to say a little more, a page or two, about the Sheep. It occurs to me I have not been entirely fair to this extraordinary creature, 'A scientific marvel!' in some people's opinion. I mean 'big-head', that's just rude, isn't it? Out of order. I should not have written it. The thing is, I do HAVE MY MOODS, that's the truth of it. Sometimes – Oh, dear! – I am up and down like a yo-yo, round and round like a revolving door, in and out like a . . . well, never mind.

Anyway (or as my old mother would say, 'Any road up'), the Sheep. Yes, she was conceited. Yes, she was a snob. But, and this is the point, she was not boring. No, sir, she knew a thing or two, that Sheep, scientific stuff mostly, gathered, I understand, from her long association with Prof Bodley. That bit I wrote earlier, for instance, 'rainbowed light *refracted* from the puddles', that was her. I would not have thought of it. She told me also, on a separate occasion, some absolutely fascinating things about spiders' webs. I have an interest in spiders. My garden's full of 'em. Anyway, spiders' webs, it turns out, are in propor- tion stronger than steel hawsers. They can stop a bee doing 20 mph dead in his tracks. Prof Bodley, it seems, among his many other researches, has produced a prototype artificial spiders' silk, thick as a washing line, that, it's rumoured, can stop an F16 *fighter aircraft* dead in its tracks. My word.

Yes, a clever character, that Sheep, maybe the cleverest, brainiest character in the entire book. Except Prof Bodley, himself, who hardly appears. Oh, yes, and except ONE OTHER, who shall be revealed. And I don't mean me. I mean, I'm not in the book, not really, am I? Or am I? I suppose, from your point of view, looking down now on the page, scratching your ear perhaps, feeling a bit peckish, I probably am. Hm . . . how peculiar, I never thought of that: an author in his own book.

Where was I? Well, not where I ought to be, that's the truth. I should be getting on with the Wolf's version by now, not lured away like some well-deceived bloodhound. This chapter is entitled, 'Space, Time and Grandma Pumfrey'. For some reason I'd got it into my head to tell you what the Sheep told me about time. 'Time,' she said, in that deep voice of hers. 'Time is what keeps everything from happening all at once.'

She said things about space too. All very interesting. All TOTALLY IRRELEVANT. And Grandma Pumfrey really belongs in the next chapter, not this. I don't know, sometimes this head of mine feels like a beehive.

Time to go home.

The Forest (again). Moonlight lay across its winding paths, illuminating its clearings, glittering on its sudden puddles and ponds. The little lamp of my bicycle added its shine to the general illumination. Dark shifting shadows crowded at the edges of my sight. Eyes blinked in the blackness. Warm, humid, mushroomy smells rose up around me. I had a rendezvous tomorrow WITH A WOLF. Something furry and alive brushed fleetingly against my cheek. I felt a sudden, irresistible desire . . . to whistle.

[6] The Wolf's Version

Do I contradict myself?
Very well then I contradict myself.
I am large, I contain multitudes.

Walt Whitman

Good morning! Pinkish sunlight in at my window. I sit here, still in my pyjamas, and review the day ahead. My spirits are once more rising. The disappointments and failures of yesterday are behind me. The mysteries and apprehensions of the forest likewise. Today, Oh yes, today I will bounce back. You, dear reader, on the other hand, I can sense it, you think we've more or less had it, don't you? That this maze, this rigmarole, this TARADIDDLE will go on, not to say multiply and expand, forever. Don't you? Yes, you do. Don't argue.

Well, be that as it may, I for my part am a terrier. Tenacity is my middle name. (Actually, it really is.) I will get at the truth of this business, you can be sure. If it is hidden, I will uncover it; buried, I'll dig it up; baked in a pie, I'll eat it (no – not that).

Anyway, on to Grandma Pumfrey's.

The Wolf. The Wolf, when I first saw him, was lolling back on an old green velvet sofa with a takeaway pizza box beside him. There was a rug on the floor, a pile of newspapers. A mirror was nailed to the back wall and a 'three little pigs' mobile suspended from the roof. The pen (or cage), which is what the Wolf was in, was situated, along with a number of others, in the garden of Grandma Pumfrey's house. A high wall enclosed the garden and security lights had been installed. The pen itself, however, did not look all that secure to me. The bars were thin, I thought, the lock and chain on the door, flimsy.

I approached and sat down on a garden chair, which Grandma Pumfrey had helpfully provided. (She, by the way, must have been the *youngest* grandma the world has ever seen. Her name was not Pumfrey either. More of this later.) The Wolf appeared to be dozing. I took up my notebook and pencil, cleared my throat and was about to speak, when –

'HEY!' yelled the Wolf.

Whereupon I, of course, leapt out of my skin.

The Wolf sat up and smiled lazily.

'Hi, there.'

He had not been dozing at all. It amused him, I rapidly discovered, to make people, er, what's the word . . .

JUMP!

See what I mean?

So, the scene is set: the walled garden; the painted wooden pen (or cage); the high blue sky with its scudding clouds; the aroma of honeysuckle (and pizza?); the racket of ducks on a nearby pond; traffic in the road.

The Wolf it turned out was in custody, under lock and key temporarily at Grandma Pumfrey's, but soon to be transferred to the local jail. Investigations were in progress. The charges, or allegations I should say, included the actual or attempted eating of Grandma Pumfrey herself, plus a number of small children, little pigs, chickens, ducks and so on. I learned much of this from the Wolf himself. He possessed, it must be said, an unusual mind, capable at one moment of confessing to or boasting of the most dreadful deeds, and at the next protesting his eternal innocence and denying everything.

Well, we talked that day on and off till late afternoon. He got me jumping now and then as I have indicated. Worse still . . . but I will come to that presently. By and large and in spite of everything, I must admit he was a surprisingly amiable witness.

So here we go. Having established the reason for my visit, I invited the Wolf to give his version of events. He was willing to do so, though what he had to say was hardly convincing. Here is a sample of our talk:

'Mr Wolf . . . recently you had occasion to travel in a cart from the McFirkins' place in the company of a Boy, a Sheep and a Lettuce.'

'If you say so.'

'What was the purpose of your journey?'

'I had some business in the town. A couple of *lunches*, that sort of thing.'

'Did you usually travel in this way, in a wood-cutter's cart?'

'Sometimes. If it suited me.'

'But how did it suit them? I mean, the

McFirkins? Their little boy and, er, you'll excuse me, a wolf.'

'I was considered trustworthy. Tame.'

'Really?'

'Yes. Raised from a cub by a forest ranger. Noble savage, faithful guardian, that sort of thing, especially of the children.'

'And were you?'

'Not really. They had me confused with some other wolf. He was the tame one. I was, er . . .

NOT!'

'I see. Must you do that? So, you were in the cart on your way to town.'

'Yes. Made myself comfortable on some sacks or cushions in the back. Read the paper.'

'What else do you remember?'

'Not much. Just the usual trip through the forest. The odd bear or robber. The Boy was a bit of a whistler, I recall. Or was it the Sheep? I may have dozed off.'

'Till you came TO THE RIVER.'

'Yes, the river. There was this teeny-weeny little row boat, I remember. Hardly room enough for its own oars. We hung around for an age while the woodcutter's lad cudgelled his brain how to get us across. Y'see –'

'According to Percy –'

'Was that his name?'

'Yes. According to him, he made a raft.'

'Not while I was there, he didn't.'

'According to the Sheep –'

'Forget the Sheep. She will only pull the wool over your eyes. Where was I? Yes, y'see, this lad was unwilling for some reason to leave me alone with the Sheep, or the Sheep alone with the Lettuce.'

'I understand that. What happened?'

'It was a puzzle, wasn't it? I solved it.'

'How?'

'Just logic, really. Tiny boat – too many passengers – it's obvious. Any self-respecting wolf would have done the same.'

'What did you do?'

'I reduced the numbers.'

'Oh, dear.'

'Yes. Ate the Sheep, ate the Boy and *rowed the boat*.' The Wolf gave me a knowing, leery smile. 'Spoilt my appetite for lunch. Rowed over anyway.'

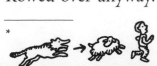

It was pleasant in the garden. Beds of white and yellow flowers bent and wavered in the breeze. There was the sound of a mower and the smell of cut grass from the other side of the wall. A small pig, I noticed, was watching me from behind a barrel.

I got to my feet, stretched my legs and began to consider this the latest and easily most ludicrous version of events. It was as full of holes as a . . . hole. Yet somehow when I challenged the Wolf, the absurdities he had described seemed, how can I explain it, to just MELT AWAY.

'So, Mr Wolf, if you ate the Sheep, how come she's still alive?'

'Different sheep. There are flocks of 'em.'

'And the Boy?'

'Twins.'

'And the Lettuce?'

'Ha! Never said I ate a lettuce. That really is ridiculous.'

Then, after I had demolished these defences, he changed tack again, firing off all manner of alibis and excuses, like a Catherine wheel.

1 All right then, they're alive. I made a little mistake.

2 I am old. I am retired. I am *reformed*.

3 My memory is going. I get mixed up with the good, er, bad old days.

4 Did you never make a mistake?

5 I have ate lots of . . . people (wry smile). I cannot be expected to remember all my meals.

Somehow, unusually for me, I kept my temper in this situation and my eye on the ball.

'Mr Wolf,' I persisted, 'Mr Wolf, surely even you must see that all this simply doesn't make sense.'

Whereupon, the Wolf shrugged and smiled again. 'You're right,' he said, and flicked his little-pigs mobile with an outstretched paw. 'I withdraw it all. Unreservedly.'

[7] A CLEARING *in the* Forest

$$E = mc^2$$
Einstein

Oh, botheration, here we go again. Back to square one. Three versions now: the Boy says this, the Sheep says that, the Wolf says the other (and withdraws it, unreservedly). But do they JOIN FORCES? Do they weave together into a

———

CARPET OF TRUTH? Do they ADD UP? They do not. If anything, they cancel each other out. I am left with less truth now than when I started. I sometimes think I would be better off writing an opera. Get all three of them – Boy, Sheep, Wolf – on stage together. Let 'em sing it out, a trio, simultaneously. Loudest wins.

This business of the truth poleaxes me at times, that's the *truth* of it. I read somewhere (George Henry Knott, I think) that 'The little knowledge we have is like a clearing in a forest', a forest which represents the unknown. The more knowledge or truth we acquire, the bigger the clearing, the greater our contact (i.e. perimeter – see diagram p.44) with the unknown. In other words, the more we know, the more we know we don't know, or if you like, the less we know. It's a puzzle. There again, as the Sheep was later to observe, 'E = mc^2, *that's* a puzzle.'

the numbers.

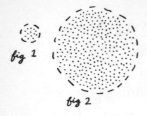

fig 1

fig 2

I don't know . . . Where was I? Oh, yes, Grandma Pumfrey's garden.

The sun was slanting down behind the house. The invisible ducks were silent on the invisible pond. The traffic, still. The aroma of cut grass mingled delightfully with a baked-bread smell issuing from Grandma Pumfrey's kitchen window. And I had finished with the Wolf. And the Wolf – Oh, dear, oh, dear! – had *not* finished with me.

I have no notes for what happened next, you will appreciate why. My memory too is unreliable. My embarrassment though is total.

How he did it, I really cannot fathom. How I was taken in, to let him OUT, beggars belief. But he charmed me, I suppose, that's it in a nutshell. I can appreciate now how smoothly he must have insinuated himself into the McFirkins' cart. And Mrs McFirkin's embarrassment. He charmed her too.

And what did he use? A smile? A confiding tone of voice? A modest request (or so it seemed)? Just to step outside for a moment. Feel the grass on his ageing feet, the breeze in his fur.

44

A fleeting freedom. Ridiculous: yes. Preposterous: absolutely. I opened the pen (or cage).

And the door flew out to meet me – smack! And I was hurtling backwards, tumbling over, bouncing against the barrel, cracking my shin on the downspout, cracking my head on . . . who knows what?

I was down and nearly out. The Wolf was out and above me. His 'smile' expanding now to something else. His hot and pizza-flavoured breath . . . his teeth. (P.S. His name, by the way, I nearly forgot to mention, was Wayne Duane 'Trustworthy' McBane, though I doubt you'll believe it.)

And then . . . from nowhere, an IMMENSE NOISE and FLASH OF LIGHT and CONCUSSION OF AIR. I was half deaf, three-quarters blind and my wits had been fairly well scattered beforehand. The looming Wolf, I sensed, was gone. And then . . . another face, pale and frowning. Oh, Grandma, what big eyes you've got! Another face, pale and . . .

There was a smell of sulphur, gunpowder perhaps . . . and bread. My nose was all there was of me still working. There was a smell of . . . *roses*? It was a puzzle all right. I could not work it out. Gave up. And fainted.

[8] Invisible Stars

Just when you least expect it,
the unexpected always happens.

Joe Orton

Where was I? Where am I? A darkened room. A bed. A bed that moves . . . up and down like the sea. Oh, my poorly head . . . I feel so dizzy. So . . . sleepy.

What's this – a bandage? What's that – the moon? Who's that? (A blurry figure at the window.) Soft rain at the window . . . I can hear it. And the curtains stirring. This is my own room . . . and bed. I am IN MY PYJAMAS.

I sleep and dream. I dream I am out in my garden pruning the roses, chopping down trees. And all the McFirkins are there with Mr McFirkin up on his ladder . . . cleaning the windows. There's a picnic.

* * *

I wake in the night with a throbbing head and a terrible thirst. There's a glass of water beside my bed. I hobble across to the window, gaze out and up at the starry sky. The stars, perhaps you know (the Sheep told me), are always with us, daytime, night-time. It's only the jealous sun that drowns or dazzles them out. I return to my bed . . . and sleep . . . and dream.

And now it's morning, late morning. I am sitting up in bed: coffee, Marmite toast, newspaper. My head still aches but I am on the mend. Up and ready (almost) for the fray, and with some ex-plaining to do. So enough of all this dreaming, dreary invalid stuff. It was only a bang on the head/shin/elbow etc. after all. Just a bit of the rough and tumble which any self-respecting investigative writer must come to expect (when he least expects) on the trail, on the spoor of, er . . . in his fearless quest for the, er . . . Where was I?

Yes, clarity, simplicity . . . What was the other one? Hm . . . let's sort things out, let's make a list, shall we? Let's make a few lists.

47

The Wolf

1 Yes, he attacked me. Sort of. Though now I suspect it was more exuberance than anything else. He leapt at the door – in case I changed my mind! – and the door did the damage. Really.

2 You see, I have developed this theory about the Wolf. He is too full of jokes and trickery. (Have you heard, they've recently removed the word 'gullible' from the dictionary? That's one of his.) He is rarely serious for two sentences together. It's my belief that his *quirky and playful* mind has held him back in his chosen career, i.e. as a wolf. You cannot very well have fun with a fellow creature you're simultaneously taking BITES OUT OF.

3 So, the Wolf: says much, does little. All the same, he is back under lock and key, you may be glad to hear.

P.S. He's also right there in the morning paper, front page, with his 'who-me?' smile and his six alibis.

Grandma Pumfrey

1   It was 'Grandma Pumfrey' back there in the garden with 'Attar of Roses' perfume PLUS SHOTGUN. That wolf, I understand, reversed into his pen or cage faster ever than he came out of it. Yes, like a bullet – Ha!

2   It was Grandma Pumfrey brought me home in her van, got me to bed, came back this morning and made my breakfast. She has left now.

3   Only well, there again in a manner of speaking, it wasn't. You see, it – NO, STOP! I WILL NOT DO THIS. I have never approved of those authors – numerous and famous, some of 'em – who deliberately set out to mystify their readers. No sir, if a man (boy, dog, chicken) has something to say, let him say it. For instance, let's fast-forward a little, shall we? I have a chapter half planned for later, entitled: *The Mystery of Professor Bodley*. Well, I can reveal to you now it will be short. The mystery remains. I never saw him. There's clarity for you.

4   As for Grandma, this is how it is: there *was* a Grandma Pumfrey, famed as vet and midwife,

only she died and left the business to her daughter. The daughter, reaching middle age and fed up with putting thermometers up cats' bottoms, took early retirement and handed over to *her* daughter. But, and this is the point, somehow the business retained its name, like Marks and Spencer. (Where's 'Marks', where's 'Spencer'?)

5   The present 'Grandma Pumfrey' is a youngish woman, mid 30s, I'd say, named, er . . . Lucy Frobisher.

What Next?

1   Good Question. Hm. It occurs to me that in some ways writing a book is like driving a car. You can only see so far down the road. Even when you know your destination – the ending! – or think you do; hills and hollows, twists and turns lie in between and obscure the view. There again, you could run out of petrol, I suppose,

suffer a puncture, get stopped for speeding – hi-jacked! No, not those. I am getting carried away. Messing up the metaphor. Where was I?

2   Yes, well, what's needed, it's obvious really, is an ACTION plan. Thus:

    i I will draw a MAP.

    ii I will make a LIST of things to DO.

    iii I will PHONE people.

    iv I will visit PERCY again.

    v I will TALK to Auntie Joyce.

    vi I will . . . hm . . . have a sip of this COFFEE.

    vii I will shut my EYES for a little, er . . . while.

    viii Zzzz.

[9] The Lettuce's Version

Cheer up! 'Tis no use to be glum boys –
'Tis written since fighting begun
That sometimes we fight and we conquer
And sometimes we fight and we run.

Thackeray

Later the same day. Here I sit in my garden reading through what I have thus far written. Oh, dear, and my moods are up and down again, like a yo-yo and all that, like the weather. (The *forecast* for the next twenty-four hours is preposterous; wait and see.) But for now the sky is clear, the sun is going down behind the trees, the air, warm and still. A team of bees is working the flower beds. A sparrow's in the bird bath. I am reading.

And so, of course, are you.* How curious. I would offer you a cup of tea, if I could, or a biscuit. Hm. My headache, you may be pleased

---

*Actually, if we're being absolutely accurate, I am *writing* 'I am reading', and you are *reading* 'I am writing'. Lovely – I like that.

to hear, has gone. The bandage has loosened a little and slides down piratically over my left eye. I must keep pushing it up. Hm.

It seems to me sometimes that I am my own worst enemy. I cannot keep this narrative of mine going in a straight line for two paragraphs together, but am forever veering off (in that car again) down some inviting country lane, ending up often as not in a ditch. There again, cheer up, as the poet says. We are what we are. A rose is a rose is a rose. Win some, lose some. His name, by the way, this poet (novelist, actually), his full name was William *Makepeace* Thackeray. There you go; no one has a monopoly on the ludicrous.

Later the same night. I sit now at the kitchen table; glass of wine, cheese and biscuits, notebook, pen. Outside fat moths thump up against the window. Frost, yes frost, sparkles on the illuminated grass. Thin AUGUST ICE, I do believe, is forming on the bird bath . . . and I am feeling somewhat foolish and fairly well pleased with myself. I have just written *The Lettuce's Version*.

No research. No journeys through the Forest. No interviews. Only for the fun of it. After all, we have heard from the others – Boy, Sheep, Wolf – so, I think to myself . . . hm, this wine's good . . . why not the Lettuce? Could things get any more absurd than they are? Story writers, so we are told (by story writers), get inside their 'characters' all the time. Pirates and witches, dark lords, elves and pixies, horses, rabbits. But who ever did a lettuce? Nobody, I'll bet.

I know, I know, this is supposed to be an investigation not a story, truth not fiction. There are no characters here, only real people, sheep and so on. All the same . . . where's that bottle? . . . it's done now. Yes, the Lettuce's Version.

Would you care to see it? Really? Are you sure? Not just being polite? Hm . . . very well then:

God in His eternal wisdom has deprived all lettuces of the power of speech. No legs either. A lettuce may not run from life's dangers, or towards life's pleasures, come to that, but must for the duration of its vegetable existence merely, er, sit there.

The Lettuce which concerns us here may well be the only really innocent party in this whole sorry tangle. The youngest too, a mere three and a half weeks. And since it cannot speak for itself, I will speak for it. Thus:

I am a Lettuce (Y'r Honour, dear readers, boys and girls), a humble lettuce, though of prize-winning stock. 'My story' as the song goes, 'is much too sad to be told' (Cole Porter), but I will tell it anyway.

On the dawning of the day in question, damp and misty, I was removed, pulled up, yanked – yes, that's the word – YANKED out of my natural element (i.e. soil) in the vegetable patch to the rear of the McFirkins' house. Whereupon, I escaped one fate: rabbits, voles, slugs (ugh!) and so forth, only to meet another.

Well, I did not feel the better for it, no sir. Flying through the air, bouncing along in some splintery box is no fun for a lettuce. I lack, as you will appreciate, any actual sense organs – eyes, ears etc. – but I am a living thing, as much as you, a sentient being. I have leaves and roots. I have a heart. I FEEL.

For instance, I could feel, on that particular morning, the motion of the cart, the atmosphere of the Forest, the flickering heat of the sun. I could feel that Sheep, too, giving me looks. What sort of looks? Sheep looks. Hm.

Worse still I had my premonitions. The situation for a vegetable or salad person on this planet is not good. Those vegetarians – smug's the word for them – have much to answer for. All this fuss they make about chickens and little lambs and never a thought for us. It is our fate, let's face it, to be EATEN. Even worse than that, consider, if you can bear to, the methods used. Baby peas frozen alive! Baby carrots boiled alive! Cabbages chopped up and steamed! It's . . .

Snow. Snow in August! I just glanced out of the window. Massive feathery flakes drifting down like . . . like parachutists. It's unheard of, amazing. Sorry, I didn't mean to interrupt – you and the Lettuce and all that – it's, well . . .

magical. Anyway, please read on, if you care to, that is. No obligation.

. . . *inhuman. Actually, the situation for we lettuces is the worst of the lot. At least* THE END, *for a tomato, say, or a radish, can have its heroic side. Like the Christians and the Lions. But a lettuce often as not just gets stuck on the side of the plate next to a steak or a pile of scampi, stuck on the side of the plate and ignored. Yes, that's the worst of the worst of it, in my opinion. I am doomed to be a* GARNISH.

However, mustn't grumble, I suppose. We are all bound to go in the end, the eaten and the eaters both. There's a cheering thought. There again, where there's life . . .

The motion of my journey at the first and for quite a while was bumpy. By and by it became smoother — some sort of road? — and, finally, following a stationary period, it pitched and rolled, rose and fell like the sea, or a river perhaps.

My whole life, as you may appreciate, is a puzzle to me. Starting out as a sleeping seed in a row of seeds, under the heavy, comforting soil, like a duvet. Then to awake and stir and grow, both ways at once, up to the radiating sun, down into the gravity of the earth, becoming in due course what I was ever meant to be: a lettuce.

Yet now this rare experience of mine, this 'journey', offered a greater puzzle still. A riddle almost. I had a sense there, on that 'river', of . . . something to be done . . . versions and possibilities. I felt – Oh, my, I have so much to tell you! I could write a book.* I could –

Sorry, me again. It's this snow, it's unbelievable. I'm outside now, wellies and anorak. It's so quiet. All the noises of the world, such as they might be at this late hour, cushioned away. My breath ghosting before me. Light from the house on the pure white lawn . . . and the phone ringing.

The phone, and it's nearly midnight. I go inside. (I *am* sorry for this second interruption; apologies to the Lettuce likewise.) Take up the receiver and a voice says: 'This is Wayne speaking.'

Wayne? It was a moment or two before I recognized my caller. More snow, dry rattling at

---

* As the song goes (Rodgers and Hart).

the window, a sheltering moth around the light bulb, puddles at my feet . . . and a pounding heart.

It was the Wolf.

[10] The Answer is IN the Cart

A child had her first ride in a lift. 'How did you like it?' asked her parent. 'It was funny,' answered the child, 'we went into a little house and the upstairs came down.'

The Paradox Box

Sentences violating Rule 7 are often ludicrous:

Being in a dilapidated condition, I was able to buy the house very cheap.

Wondering irresolutely what to do next, the clock struck twelve.

As a mother of five with another on the way, my ironing board is always up.
William Strunk Jnr

> Babies haven't any hair
> Old men's heads are just as bare
> Between the cradle and the grave
> Lies a haircut and a shave.

Samuel Hoffenstein*

_____

*Yes, I know, I've overdone it here. The thing is, I do love a good quote and was pretty desperate to shoe horn all three of 'em in somewhere, and was running out of chapters. I especially like the William Strunk, it's from a really useful little book on English grammar and so forth, *The Elements of Style*. I read it all the time. And Strunk, of course, is such an ace name, wouldn't you say? Better even than Smout.

I should stop. This will make a funny-looking page; hardly room for the story, which, I've just remembered, is teetering on the brink. Suspense is in the air, and I am, well . . . I am IN THE WAY. Sorry about *that*. Exit.

The Wolf. The Wolf was phoning from the jail. Allowed one call, he had chosen at this mad hour, to phone *me*. Apparently, I was, wait for it, ON HIS CONSCIENCE. On his menu more like.

'I just had to talk to you,' (said he), 'about the accident.'

'Accident? Ah, yes, where you were trying to eat me.'

'No, no.'

'Yes, yes. It was a vicious attack.'

'High spirits.'

'Low cunning. I have the lumps to prove it.'

'Listen to me.' The Wolf lowered his voice. 'I have this reputation, all wolves do, but in my case it's undeserved. I never (almost inaudible), well hardly ever, ate a single soul. It's my quirky and playful nature. I make things up . . . for the fun of it.'

'Fun? I was knocked flying.'

'It's true. You were struck down, by the door mainly, and I am truly sorry for it.'

All this, of course, only confirmed my earlier speculations (see page 48). There again, that was theory, this was reality. I had a wolf on the end of the line and my hands were sweating.

Where was I? Ah yes . . . truly sorry for it.

Silence for a while plus a sound like a (counterfeit) sob.

'Which is why I called.'

My turn for silence.

'I wanted to make it up to you.'

Silence number three.

'It's about that business in the cart you were so interested in.'

Cart? Cart? For a split second I could not fathom what he was on about. (How far I had strayed from my original enterprise.)

'You remember: me, the Boy, the Sheep?'

'And the Lettuce.'

'Yeah. Anyway, listen, I have a clue for you. You are looking for the truth, right? A reliable witness and all that. So – are you still there?'

'More or less.' I was weary and unenthusiastic. I would not put my trust in wolves.

'So, here's the clue: *the answer is in the cart.*'

Now there was a commotion back in the jail. I could hear other voices, clattering sounds and heavy breathing. Growls!

'Just a minute.' The Wolf was speaking to someone else (the warder?). 'I'm almost done.' And then to me, 'Sorry about that. Time's nearly up. Where was I?'

'You had a clue?' Despite myself, a tiny candle of hope had begun to gleam.

'Oh, yeah – listen. Go and talk to the little sister.'

'Rosalind? She wasn't in the cart.'

'That's all you know. Go and talk to her.'

Suddenly, a tremendous drumming down the phone. I had to hold it away from my ear.

'What's *that?*'

'Nothing much. Some old Troll making a pest of himself.'

'Troll?'

'Yeah. They've got all sorts in here. Not to worry though.' The Wolf gave a laugh. 'I'll be out soon; there's no real evidence against me.' And he spluttered again with laughter. 'I ate it all.'

[11] Little Sister

The sun was rising and so was I. Yes, sir, I was back in business, back on the trail, back in the saddle, back to front (yes, probably). Anyway, my spirits, ludicrously, were on the up. Charmed and persuaded again by a WOLF, I was out and off once more to the McFirkins' place. On foot. The appropriately inappropriate weather conditions did not favour cycling.

I made a detour to the county jail. No sign of trouble. No trolls. (There are no trolls.) The thing is, by the end of that phone call the Wolf – how ever does he do it? – had got *me* worrying about *his* welfare. I dropped off a small pie (meat and potato) and a pack of cards at the warder's office.

* * *

64

The Forest. I am with young Percy in this matter. It has to be my favourite place too. And on this particular morning – Oh, my! Low sunlight slanting through the shrouded trees. The whole place moulded together by snow. Total whiteness, only here and there splashes of colour from the thaw that had already begun. It was like a picture in a colouring book, hardly started.

I walked, crunching and sloshing through the crisp(stroke)melting snow. My thoughts, this beehive head again, were everywhere. The beauty of the scene; the questions I would put to little Rosalind; the reliability of the Wolf. All the same, my heart was lifted. There and then I vowed to stick to my task, come what may. No more distractions, diversions, 'country lanes' – no, sir! The truth WAS out there and I would hunt it down. (I stuck my chest out, lengthened my stride.) It's all so easy, forest or not, to lose your way. The potential ramifications of a book, for instance (i.e. this one), are mind-boggling. (But I will resist them.) Yes, even as I write this sentence – word – LETTER – I am thinking (left, right and centre) about . . . sentences already written (see above), and those still yet to come (p.t.o.); errors and omissions; paper, pen and ink – and the printing (if I'm lucky) down the line – jacket, blurb and bar code. Plus, all the while, a separate stream or swarm of thought: the Forest. I see a cat – a polecat? – slinking along. Some brilliantly coloured birds – finches? – parrots? I see, most definitely, a man with a wriggling sack. I see . . .

Where was I? Well, in serious danger of BREAKING MY VOW no sooner than it's made, that's where. Sorry about that. My mistake. There again, nobody's perfect . . . not even you. So don't be so quick to criticize others. 'Judge not, that ye be not judged' (Holy Bible). Besides, I'm doing all the work, all you have to do is sit there. Or stand, I suppose (in a book shop – not buying!). Or lie . . . reading in bed is popular . . . or in the bath. I could do with a bath. Hm.

I arrived at the McFirkins' house shortly after nine-thirty. Mrs McFirkin was in the yard with a mighty axe, making firewood. She stood within a circle of flying woodchips. A nervous little dog sat watching her, just out of range. Observing Mrs McFirkin's strength and effort, I was, in a flash, in a microsecond, reminded of my mother; how strong *she* was. How I'd come home from school sometimes to find whole wardrobes moved and carpets laid.

Well, it turned out Percy and his dad were not at home. Gone to a football match, apparently, in the next town. No snow there. (So would they believe in ours?) Little Rosalind was up in her room in bed with a sore throat. I accepted a mug of tea from Mrs McFirkin, chatted impatiently a while . . . and climbed the stairs.

Rosalind was sitting up in bed with glasses on the end of her nose, a shawl round her shoulders and a huge book open on her lap. She looked like a little old grandma, except, that is, for a crowd of soft toys, teddies and such, tucked in beside her. The book was the *Shorter Oxford Dictionary* (Volume II, Marl – Z and Addenda).

Rosalind heaved it shut and gave me a welcoming smile.

In the urgency of the moment, not pausing even to ask how she was, I plunged straight in.

'Rosalind, do you remember when I was here last week, talking to Percy?'

'Yes.' A gruff little voice.

'And you were in the hammock, and Percy was telling about his adventures in the cart, and the river and all that?'

'Yes.'

'Well, the thing is . . . where were *you* then?'

'In the hammock.'

'No, I mean, when he was in the cart, where were you?'

Rosalind hesitated and glanced towards the door. Then, '*I* was in the cart.'

'Ah!' And all in a rush, instantaneously, I thought, 'A witness – a true witness!' and, 'The Wolf was right!' and, 'Now we'll get to the bottom of this!' and, 'Why the *Shorter Oxford*?' and . . . a few other things.

Faintly from the rear of the house came the rhythmic sound of Mrs McFirkin's marathon wood-chopping. Later she would bundle up the firewood with loops of wire and stack the bundles in the woodshed. Later still, go off and sell them.

Rosalind and I continued our (for my part) urgent conversation. She was quite willing to give me her version of events. Just didn't want her mother to hear.

'I was supposed to be going to my friend's house. Only I got a lift with Percy and –'

'Percy said you were still in your nightie waving him goodbye.'

'No, I was right next to him. Between the Lettuce and the Wolf.'

'And the Sheep . . .?'

'On the blankets in the back.'

Rosalind gave a little cough and helped herself to a spoonful of pink medicine from a bottle beside the bed. Later on she sucked a lozenge.

Well, as you can imagine, the questions were stacking up in my head like aeroplanes waiting to land. I hardly knew what to ask next.

'How come the Wolf was, er . . .' I paused, not wanting to scare my witness witless, but she was ahead of me.

'He talked his way in. Something about a sick cousin in hospital.'

'Percy said he was going to the vet's.'

'No, hospital. He was carrying a bunch of flowers. Afterwards Mummy said he "insinuated" himself.'

'Did she? . . . Ah!'

I pressed on with my enquiries. The prospect of so much TRUTH so readily available had got me feeling wildly cheerful, DELIRIOUS almost. I was like a child let loose in a SWEET SHOP.

Rosalind spoke of the journey through the Forest, confirming this – the eye-patch man, the pear tree; denying that – tigers, trolls, bandits. It was her own idea to stay with Percy and not go to her friend's. The trip excited her and she wanted to see the river. Also, at the horticultural show – whence the Lettuce, via Auntie Joyce, was headed – they had demonstrations of rural crafts (and candyfloss), so she had heard.

I studied my small companion as we conversed. I had the curious feeling that I was watching a five-year-old (four and three-quarters, actually) and hearing a twenty-five-year-old. She looked like Percy – reddish hair, round face, freckles – and sounded like . . . like Bertrand Russell. You may recall (Chapter 5, page 32), my mentioning how clever the Sheep was, and how in the entire book there was only one cleverer. Well, here she is: IQ 160+, little Rosalind McFirkin take a bow.

Oh, yes, Rosalind was the ace witness all right, of all time. Clarity, Simplicity, Concision, she had the lot. Only – Oh, no! (Why is there always something?) – her little voice, even as I admired its logical, plausible flow, was fading, with tickling cough and growing gruffness, fading towards (I leant closer, closer) in . . . audi . . . bility.

And then – Oh, no again! – in came Mrs McFirkin, warm-faced and smelling like a sawmill. Rosalind would not tell what she knew – we had got to the river – in her mother's presence. Mrs McFirkin judged Rosalind should come downstairs and rest her poorly throat. I . . . was speechless.

Outside a massive thaw was in progress. Half the snow had gone, hot sunlight glittered on the rest and the water barrels were overflowing. Mrs McFirkin led the way to the kitchen. I followed on with Rosalind's duvet. Rosalind came last with a book in her hand.

In the hallway she tapped my arm and whispered, 'Sorry about the . . .'

'It's all right.'

'I know you really want to know what (cough, cough!) happened.'

'Don't worry, I'll –'

'The difficulty is, I can't (cough) tell you . . .'

We entered the kitchen. Already Mrs McFirkin was peering into the fridge.

'. . . just now.' Rosalind smiled. 'But you could read it, if you like.' And pressed into my hand the book she was holding . . .

'Ice cream?' called Mrs McFirkin over her shoulder. 'Sorbet? Juice?'

. . . and a tiny golden key.

[12] A Book in a Book!

YYUR
YYUB
ICUR
YY4ME*

With trembling fingers I turned the key in the lock of Rosalind's diary. It proved to be a remarkable piece of work for a five-year-old. Page after page of the neatest, tiniest writing you ever saw or squinted at, with hardly a crossing out or spelling mistake. Like a Mozart manuscript. It was a fat little book with a double page for each day and a scattering of 'fascinating facts', puzzles and so forth (see above*).

Of course, the temptation to read more than I was entitled to was great. There again, the urge to GET ON WITH IT was greater. Rosalind's entry for the day in question – the Red Letter Day – began as follows:

> Got up early. Had sausages for breakfast. Helped Percy with his Frog Island. Packed my bag to go to Hanna's house. Found Horace's hat.

Well, in my UNDERSTANDABLE and frantic haste, I skipped a bit here: the loading of the cart and so forth (I had heard that enough times, and SO HAVE YOU), the trail through the forest (ditto), until (I thought I would explode!) once more (and perhaps *finally*) we reached THE RIVER.

> Percy found this little boat and rowed over with the Sheep. And rowed back. And took the Wolf over. And brought the Wolf back. And took the Lettuce over. And brought the Lettuce back. And kicked his football for a while. And read his comic. And remembered the Sheep – she was 'Baaing!' And fetched her back.
>
> I stopped Horace from drinking too much at the river. And gave him his nosebag. The Sheep was silent and standoffish. The Wolf – said his name was Waldteufel, but I knew it was Wayne – was being silly and pretending to eat everybody. Percy played football for a while with me in goal. And fell asleep.

I was reading this in the barn, out of sight, I hoped, of Mrs McFirkin. Great slabs of snow were shifting and sliding from the roof, crashing to the ground, exploding back into flakes again, or so it seemed. The air was humid, steamy almost; a most peculiar combination of weather. There was a large tin bath on the floor in the far corner, I noticed, full of water and a log maybe, with things moving in it.

Oh, the speed of human thought, as fast as light, I guess. Even as my eyes were racing over Rosalind's pages, my mind was picturing the scene: the grass right down to the water's edge, the expanse of the river with morning light upon it, flickering triangles of whiteness, hints of rainbow colours, and the town on the other side.

And I could SEE them, yes! This curious, unlikely gang: Boy, Wolf, Sheep (Lettuce), lolling

around on the bank, pausing, as it were, in their lives. And little Rosalind, with her quick mind and speed of thought, about to *sort them out* (I'd guessed that much) and set them going again. And so it proved.

> I *had a talk with Percy (woke him up).*
> I *said, 'Take the Sheep over first.'*
> He *said, 'Done that already.'*
> I *said, 'Then take the Wolf over . . .'*
> He *said, 'Done that.'*
> I *said, '. . . and* bring the Sheep back.'
> He *said, 'Huh?'*
> I *said, 'Then take the Lettuce over . . .'*
> He *said (laughing), 'Yeah – got it!'*
> I *said, '. . . and* come back for the Sheep.'
> And he *said, 'Yippee!' and booted, by mistake,*
> his *ball into the river. And never minded.*

So there we have it. I feel I should be opening a BOTTLE OF CHAMPAGNE. The Riddle's End (see diagram). You knew the answer, already, of course, as we all do, but never till now had any notion, I'll bet, of WHO FOUND IT FIRST. Or the circumstances. The details. The larger, denser, altogether more complicated TRUTH of it. Now you do.

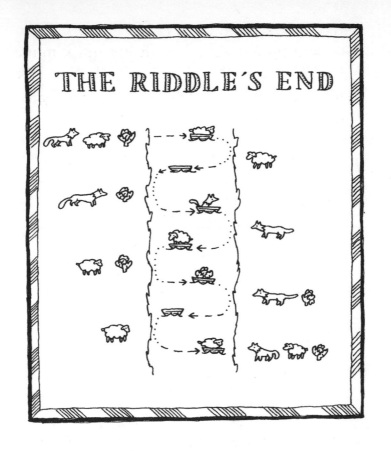

THE RIDDLE'S END

OK, so it's not so very different, you might say, from what you *already* knew. A lot of words (14,096 of 'em) to little purpose. Naturally, you are entitled to your opinion, if it is your opinion, though I do sincerely hope that in this particular instance you may just possibly be just ever so slightly . . .

WRONG!

Where was I? Rosalind. Rosalind waved her brother out of sight, giving up, it seems, on her ambition to attend the horticultural show, and drove the cart with Horace (he knew the way all on his own) to her friend's house. And stayed the night.

I sat in the barn. Closed and locked the diary. Heard an intriguing 'Plop!' from the tin bath. Went to investigate. It was Percy's 'Frog Island', a smudgy label on the side said as much. An arrangement of logs with a covering of moss and twigs. An unlikely collection of plastic cowboys, dinosaurs, bits of Lego. A tiny home-made match-box boat tied up at one end. A wind-up bath-toy duck. And in the water and on the island a flurry of little frogs. Full of their own concerns, I have no doubt. That duck for one.

I stepped outside, blinking in the brighter light. Mrs McFirkin was somewhere not far off with a chainsaw. I made my way to the house.

[13] Errors and Omissions

Truth is truth, be it written in the sky
or on a Weetabix box.

George Henry Knott

We think we know and we don't know. We think we don't know and we do. *I* think . . . I sort of half maybe or three-quarters nearly perhaps know . . . something. How about you? Do you at least know more than you did, would you say? I am not expecting you to be enlightened. Lies, confusion and doubt *are* all around us. *The Boy, the Wolf, the Sheep and the Lettuce*, what is it, after all? Just my little 'clearing in the forest'. I have done what I can.

It is a few days later, by the way, late afternoon. I am back in my beloved garden, in the deckchair taking my ease. This garden of mine, this time of year, is like a green cup from which I hardly can see out. I have a barbecue going. Company expected. Where was I?

Yes . . . done what I can. Look at it this way. The World, the Universe, or at least that bit of it that we have knowledge or an *inkling* of, is surely (or possibly) composed of time and space, of course, and STUFF. And all the . . . grass, and all the roses, deckchairs and wine bottles, boats and bridges, mushrooms and men with wriggling sacks, and the sacks likewise, and the 'wriggling', and tigers and trolls (except there are no trolls), wood smoke, twittering bats, baby frogs, baby carrots, and lettuces, sheep and wolves, and golden afternoon light, and me and you ARE the STUFF. And all of us forever on the move, like a million, billion billiard balls. No wonder it's a puzzle. 'No disgrace'*, is it? Not to solve it, I mean.

Which brings me to some errors and omissions. The promised map, you'll note, has not materialized. It did not seem useful when I thought about it. The talk with Auntie Joyce did take place, but wasn't interesting so I left it out.

———

*And come at last to that glad place
Where puzzlement is no disgrace,
And mind it not, nor think it odd
(A riddle may confound a God!)
Sarah Osgood Grover

Sorry, Auntie! I never finished telling you the Lettuce's version, and never will. The offer of cups of tea, (see page 52) was, I have since realized, unwise. This book, my publisher advises, could easily become a bestseller, 300,000 copies, say, which even at 20p a cup could cost me . . . £60,000. So, offer withdrawn.

Anyway, there's a few (errors and omissions). Should you spot any more, as I fear you may, please DON'T write to me. I am happy IN ADVANCE to take your word (without your word, so to speak) and withdraw it, whatever it is . . . unreservedly.

Which brings me to . . . hang on, I've just remembered, the biggest omission of the lot. How could I have (nearly) forgotten it?

Multiverses

The idea is simple enough, once you have the Sheep explain it to you. We've all heard of the Universe, right? (See above.) Well, the theory is, so the Sheep says, perhaps there could be more than one, loads of 'em, in fact, *Multiverses*, i.e. one for each version of the truth. So in one particular time and place with one particular load of stuff, Percy did build a raft, the Wolf did get to eat everybody, the Lettuce was Queen of the May or whatever. Truth, in other words, is just another variable and all argument or INVESTI-GATION of any sort whatsoever is unnecessary.

I cannot say I like the sound of this. Where would it end? The donkey (Horace) could be a mule, the frogs toads, day night. In some universe or other the sky is always starry (the sun never rises). And the Wolf or Rosalind wrote this book and I'm a bit player. Or you wrote it, and I am reading it . . . NOW.

So, anyway: Multiverses, that was the big omission, really big. Except, of course, that now, in this universe, it gets to be included. Ha!

Well, there we are, time for farewells, I think. Thank you for your kind attention. Sorry if I YELLED a bit in places, or got worked up, or even, heaven forbid, was RUDE. Time to write, 'The End'. Time to get a move on with this barbecue. I should start cooking soon. Bring things out from the kitchen. Put my apron on. Prepare to greet my . . . Oh, look, here she is now – green dress, straw hat, glad smile – opening the garden gate and calling my name.

[14] The Spider in the Rose

And who are you? Said he.
Don't puzzle me, said I.
Laurence Sterne

It is late. Lucy, my saviour with a shotgun, has gone home. She really is, I am discovering, a most delightful companion: good-humoured, capable, kind. How lucky I was to meet her. And I owe it all to a wolf. Hm.

Where was I? Yes . . . it's late. Lucy has gone and the barbecue is cooling down. Glimmers of light still flicker in the garden, stars shine and I am here transfixed . . . watching spiders.

An hour ago while clearing up, I came upon this little mass of spiders' eggs just on the point of hatching. Out they came and off they went, amazing specks of curious and puzzled life, hundreds of 'em. And the breeze caught some and blew them around. Others got no further than the flower pot they emerged in. And now here's one of them, ascending step by step (times eight!) the stem of a rose, overhanging my deckchair, overhanging my head. A rose is not a simple flower, you know. Its convolutions are remarkable, like Russian dolls (a rose in a rose in a rose). And up and up and into it, at last the tiny spiderling proceeds. Its near-invisible legs negotiating the hairy surface of a petal. Over the ragged edge of the rose and out of sight. Its investigations, you might say, have just begun. What will it find?

[15] Down the Road

I'm going into the next room to pack my bags
and you'll never see me again, except at mealtimes
and odd moments during the day and night
for a cup of tea and a bun.

Ionesco

Every good book, so we're told, has a beginning, a middle and an end. In which case this must be a very good book. It has two beginnings, a multitude of middles and no end of ends. Here's another.*

The trouble is, the previous endings — roses and romance and all that — simply won't do. I should've remembered. Children have no patience with that sort of thing. I was a child myself once (preposterous thought). Watching old cowboy or pirate movies, groaning whenever the hero broke off from slaughter to embrace — Oh, yuck! — the heroine. Human affection came a poor third to mayhem and murder for me in those days, and kissing was nowhere.

---

* I know, I'm overdoing it again and should STOP — and
  I will, I will!

Incidentally, if it's action you're looking for in a book, watch out for the works of Wayne Duane McBane. Yes, in recent years the Wolf has taken up his pen; thrillers and courtroom dramas mostly. The conclusion of his first ('Reader, I ate him!') was particularly admired. I have not read them myself. The Sheep, too, has entered the pages of a book, another book, that is: an account of her remarkable origins. Turns out she *was* a scientific marvel, a CLONE in fact. Apparently, there's not just one of her now, but dozens. Pity the poor sheepdogs – Ha!

And now I'll stop, I really will. Mrs Smout (guess who?) is waving at me from the garden. We're off to take the baby for a stroll; a walk in the Forest. Tea at the McFirkins', perhaps . . .

P.S. If I think of anything else, I'll put it in a SEQUEL. Goodbye, goodbye! EXIT.

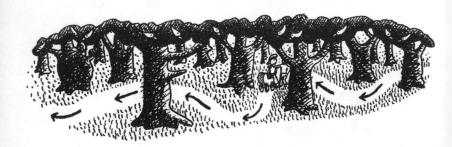

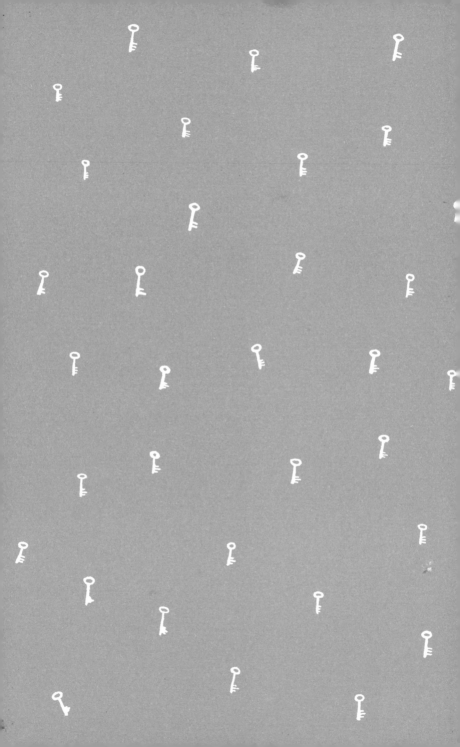